SACRAMENTO PUBLIC LIBRARY
828 "I" Street
Sacramento, CA 95814
06/20

D0031475

The LAST FIREHAWK

The Silver Swamp

by
Katrina Charman

SCHOLASTIC INC.

The LAST FIREHAWK

Read All the Books

1. The Last Firehawk — The Ember Stone

2. The Last Firehawk — The Crystal Caverns

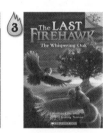

3. The Last Firehawk — The Whispering Oak

4. The Last Firehawk — Lullaby Lake

5. The Last Firehawk — The Shadowlands

6. The Last Firehawk — The Battle for Perodia

7. The Last Firehawk — The Cloud Kingdom

8. The Last Firehawk — The Silver Swamp

9. The Last Firehawk — The Golden Temple

More books coming soon!

scholastic.com/lastfirehawk

Table of Contents

For Maddie, Piper, and Riley. –KC
For Lili and Zaza. –JT

If you purchased this book without a cover, you should be aware that this book is stolen property. It was reported as "unsold and destroyed" to the publisher, and neither the author nor the publisher has received any payment for this "stripped book."

Copyright © 2020 by Katrina Charman
Illustrations by Judit Tondora copyright © 2020 by Scholastic Inc.

All rights reserved. Published by Scholastic Inc., *Publishers since 1920.*
SCHOLASTIC, BRANCHES, and associated logos are trademarks and/or registered trademarks of Scholastic Inc.

The publisher does not have any control over and does not assume any responsibility for author or third-party websites or their content.

No part of this publication may be reproduced, stored in a retrieval system, or transmitted in any form or by any means, electronic, mechanical, photocopying, recording, or otherwise, without written permission of the publisher. For information regarding permission, write to Scholastic Inc., Attention: Permissions Department, 557 Broadway, New York, NY 10012.

This book is a work of fiction. Names, characters, places, and incidents are either the product of the author's imagination or are used fictitiously, and any resemblance to actual persons, living or dead, business establishments, events, or locales is entirely coincidental.

Library of Congress Cataloging-in-Publication Data

Names: Charman, Katrina, author. | Tondora, Judit, illustrator.
Title: The Silver Swamp / by Katrina Charman ; [illustrated by Judit Tondora]
Description: New York : Branches/Scholastic Inc., [2020] | Series: The last firehawk ; [8] | Summary: When Blaze is captured by giant birds, Tag and Skyla search the Cloud Kingdom for her, including the dangerous Silver Swamp, with only their magical map as a guide.
Identifiers: LCCN 2019028613 | ISBN 9781338565317 (paperback) | ISBN 9781338565324 (library binding) | ISBN 9781338565331 (ebook)
Subjects: CYAC: Owls—Fiction. | Squirrels—Fiction. | Animals, Mythical—Fiction. | Magic—Fiction. | Adventure and adventurers—Fiction. | Fantasy.
Classification: LCC PZ7.1.C495 Sil 2019 | DDC [Fic]—dc23
LC record available at https://lccn.loc.gov/2019028613

10 9 8 7 6 5 4 3 2 1   20 21 22 23 24

Printed in China   62

First edition, June 2020
Illustrated by Judit Tondora
Edited by Rachel Matson
Book design by Maria Mercado

⤬ INTRODUCTION ⤬

Tag, a small barn owl, his friends Skyla, a squirrel, and Blaze, a firehawk, are in the magical land of the Cloud Kingdom. They are searching for clues to find Blaze's family: the lost firehawks. But all is not what it seems in this new world.

Blaze has been kidnapped by giant birds and taken to their nest in the tall trees. With the help of three golden feathers, the Ember Stone, and their magical map, Tag and Skyla must find and rescue their friend. But this journey is not going to be easy. To find Blaze, Tag and Skyla must travel through the dark and dangerous Silver Swamp. Strange creatures lurk around every corner, and a mysterious dark smudge has been appearing on the magical map. Someone—or *something*—is following them.

The adventure continues . . .

THE CLOUD

Golden Temple

Snappers Stream

Twisty Trees

Crystal Pass

N W O E S

KINGDOM

Ice Mountains

Rainbow Waterfall

Silver Swamp

THE UNUSUAL FLOWERS

Tag and Skyla stood in a dusty clearing and examined the magical map. The ground felt like sand beneath their feet. It twinkled in the sunlight.

4

Skyla pointed to a group of tall trees on the map. The trees stood in the middle of an island, surrounded by dark water. She read the label, "Silver Swamp."

"It looks like that's where the giant birds' nests are!" Tag said.

Skyla nodded. "I wonder why they call it the Silver Swamp?"

"I guess we're going to find out," Tag said. "Let's go." He tucked the map into his sack.

The sun shined bright as they walked along a dusty path.

"I hope Blaze is okay," Skyla said.

"I hope so too," Tag replied. "But she is strong and brave. And she has her special firehawk powers."

A little way ahead, Tag could see a clearing. The ground was covered in brightly colored, unusual-looking flowers. Tag gasped. The flowers were like nothing he had ever seen before. Some grew taller than him. Others shone pink and green and yellow neon colors. They glowed like fireflies.

"Look at that!" Skyla exclaimed. She ran over and stood beneath a huge mushroom. It towered over her like a giant umbrella.

Skyla sniffed a bell-shaped flower, then reached out to touch its petals when—

PUFFFF!

A spray of sparkly purple glitter shot out of the flower. It covered Skyla's face and fur.

"Skyla!" Tag called, rushing over to her. "Are you okay?"

"Achooo!" Skyla sneezed. "I'm okay. This stuff is just so sticky!"

She brushed at the glitter, but it stuck to her fur.

Tag laughed.
"You look super
sparkly!"

Skyla rolled her
eyes as she kept
brushing her fur.

Tag pulled out
the map to check they were going the right
way. The magical golden feathers had drawn
this map of the Cloud Kingdom. Now, each
time Tag and Skyla looked at it, it changed
to show them where they were. Two small
figures stood on the map in the middle of the
colorful clearing. They looked just like Skyla
and Tag.

"That's us," Skyla said, pointing at the
tiny figures.

"Don't touch the paper with your sticky
paw!" Tag warned. "You'll make the map
all glittery!"

Skyla huffed and continued walking.

Tag was about to follow her, but something caught his eye on the map. He frowned as he took a closer look. The dark smudge was back. And this time it was even darker.

"Skyla," Tag said. "What do you think *this* is?" But then—

A rustling sound came from the trees behind him.

Tag pulled out his dagger.

INTO THE DARK

The rustling sound continued.

"Do you hear that?" he whispered to Skyla. She stopped walking and turned back toward Tag.

"Hear what?" Skyla asked.

Tag looked around, but he couldn't see anyone in the nearby trees.

Skyla held up her slingshot. "What's wrong?" she asked.

"The black smudge is back on the map," he whispered. "I heard something in the trees. I think we are being followed." Tag thought about the dark figure he thought he had seen when they'd arrived in the Cloud Kingdom.

Skyla narrowed her eyes and looked toward the trees.

"I don't see anyone," she said. "It's probably just the wind."

Tag was sure that he had heard something, but Skyla was right. There was no one in the trees.

Maybe that strange dark smudge on the map is just making me feel jumpy? Tag thought.

"Let's stay on our guard," he told Skyla. "We don't know what new dangers we might discover."

As they walked, the path became wider and wider. Tag noticed that the ground was becoming damp and muddy.

"Watch out," Skyla called from a little way ahead. "There are some big puddles."

The farther they walked, the wetter and muddier the ground became. Their feet squelch, squelch, squelched in the mud. It came up to their ankles.

"This must be the swamp," Tag said.

"I wish Blaze was here, so she could fly me over this. I really hate getting wet," Skyla grumbled. She held her tail in the air to keep it dry.

"Me too," Tag said. "I'm too small to carry you on my back, but we'll walk through it together—" He stopped suddenly.

Just a moment before, they had been walking in the sun. But now, it was as if someone had turned out the lights.

Skyla noticed too. "Tag! It's so dark!"

"What just happened?" Tag asked. "It was daytime just a second ago."

Skyla pointed to the sky. Tag gazed up. A huge silver moon shone above. It was twice the size of the moon in Perodia. It was like a shiny coin in the sky.

Tag examined the map. "Hmmm," he said. "Look at this." He pointed at a picture of the sun on one side of the map.

"That's where we came from," Skyla said.

Then Tag pointed to the Silver Swamp. On that side of the map was a picture of the moon.

Silver Swamp

"Maybe that side of the Cloud Kingdom is always light," Skyla said, "and this side is always dark."

Tag put the map back in his sack and felt a shiver run through his feathers. In the dark, it would be harder to see if danger was close by. He thought of the dark smudge again.

"Tag!" Skyla cried. She held out her slingshot, her eyes wide.

Two dark figures stood a little way ahead in the trees, staring at them.

THE STRANGERS

Tag pulled out his dagger and moved closer to Skyla.

The two dark figures watched them.

"Do you think they are dangerous?" whispered Skyla. Tag could feel her fur shaking.

"I'm not sure," Tag said. "They could be friendly."

Tag and Skyla crept forward. The strangers did the same.

Tag narrowed his eyes. There was something familiar about these figures.

"Look," Skyla said. "One of them has a slingshot, just like me."

"The other has a dagger like mine," Tag whispered.

He stood as tall as he could. "Who are you?" he shouted, trying to sound brave.

His voice echoed around the trees.

"Who are you . . . you . . . you . . ." a voice echoed back.

"I'm Tag," Tag replied. "This is Skyla. We're searching for our friend."

"Friend . . . friend . . . friend . . ." the strange voice repeated.

"Maybe they are trying to tell us they are friendly?" Skyla guessed. She lowered her slingshot, and the stranger did the same.

Tag walked closer to the figures, then he laughed.

Skyla put her paws on her hips. "What's so funny?" she asked.

"They look like us because they *are* us!" Tag laughed. He held out a wing to one of the strangers, and the stranger copied the action. "They are our reflections!"

The tree trunks were silver and the moonlight shone off them, turning them into shiny mirrors. All around, Tag and Skyla could see their reflections staring back at them.

"Look at the water," Tag said. "It's silver like the trees."

Skyla grinned and gave her reflection a high five. Her paw sparkled in the light. "Ugh, you were right, Tag," she said. "I'm still so glittery!"

They walked on, zigzagging through the silvery trees. Soon, there was more water than solid ground.

"How deep do you think this water will get?" Skyla asked, worried. "You know I can't swim."

The silvery water was almost up to her waist now. "There might be something under there, waiting to bite us," she added.

"We've still got a way to go until we reach the tall trees," Tag said, wishing there was a quicker way to cross the swamp. He thought about flying ahead, but he couldn't leave Skyla behind.

CROAK! CROAK!

"What was that?" Skyla asked. She grabbed her slingshot.

Tag pulled out his dagger again. Even with the big, bright moon, it was hard to see.

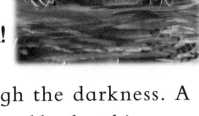

CROAK! CROAK! CROAK!

Tag peered through the darkness. A hundred small eyes peered back at him.

CHAPTER 4

THE SWAMP

"Run, Skyla!" Tag yelled.

SPLASH! SPLASH! SPLASH! Tag and Skyla ran through the silvery water as quickly as they could. But the bright-eyed creatures crawled closer and closer.

Tag and Skyla stood back-to-back in the water as the creatures surrounded them. Tag's wing shook as he held his dagger. The moonlight reflected off of the tree trunks onto the water below.

Hundreds of toads stared up at Tag and Skyla.

"There are so many of them!" Tag said.

He wished that Blaze was here. Her powers were so strong. She would be able to scare them away with her cry, or blast them with a fireball. He and Skyla only had their weapons.

The toads croaked and splashed around in front of them, but they didn't seem to be coming any closer.

"What are they doing?" Skyla asked.

Tag scratched his head. "I'm not sure. They're not looking at *us* anymore."

He stepped toward a large, balloon-shaped toad sitting on a log floating nearby.

"Hello," Tag said.

The toad stared at Tag. "Hello!" it croaked.

Then it stuck out its long tongue, and **PLOP!** It jumped into the water to join its friends.

Tag sighed and put his dagger away.

"They are just normal toads," he said. "I don't think they'll hurt us."

"I think they are playing," Skyla added.

She put her paw on a log and some of the sticky glitter on her fur came off onto it. "Excuse me," she said to a nearby toad, "we're looking for our friend. Can you help us find—"

CROAK!

The toad jumped away from Skyla.

"Huh," Skyla said. "I guess he didn't want to talk."

She turned to another group of toads. "Can any of you help us find our friend?" she asked.

"Get away!" the toads croaked. They quickly swam off.

"Wait!" Skyla called. "We won't hurt you."

"What was that all about? Those toads left in a hurry," Tag said.

Skyla shrugged. "Maybe we scared them."

Tag frowned. *The first toad I talked to hadn't seemed scared*, he thought. *Something is not right . . .*

Suddenly, a large toad popped its head up out of the water. It looked at Skyla, then Tag.

"Danger!" the toad croaked.

Then it and all the other toads leaped away from Tag and Skyla as fast as they could hop.

"Come back!" Tag called after the toads. "Where is the danger?"

He held out his dagger, searching for danger. But the toads had gone and the swamp was still and silent.

"Get ready," Tag told Skyla. "If danger is coming, we need to be ready to fight."

SKYLA'S IDEA

Tag and Skyla held out their weapons.
They continued on their way, looking around
nervously. But no new dangers appeared.

"We should stop to eat," Tag suggested
after a while. "We'll need our energy to get
the rest of the way through this swamp."

Skyla nodded. "Good idea. I'm hungry."

They sat on a fallen log, then ate some berries and drank some water.

"I wish we could move faster," Skyla said. "Blaze needs us, and this swampy water is really slowing us down."

"But how can we move faster?" Tag asked. "You can't fly without Blaze."

"I've got an idea!" Skyla grinned. She pulled at some vines hanging overhead. "Help me with these vines."

Tag helped pull down the vines. Then he watched as Skyla twisted them together.

Tag smiled. "You're making a raft!" he said. "Just like at Lullaby Lake."

Skyla nodded. "We will move quicker on top of the water. *And* we won't get wet!"

Tag found two large sticks. "We can use these to steer the raft," he said.

When the raft was finished, he and Skyla climbed on.

"It's a bit wobbly," Skyla said, "but it will do. Which way?"

Tag pulled out the map, being careful not to get it wet. The small pictures of him and Skyla were right in the middle of Silver Swamp. "That way," he said. "We should reach the tall trees soon."

Together, they steered the raft across the water. Tag could hear the toads croaking far behind them. His stomach flipped over, wondering what the toads had been so afraid of. *Hopefully we are leaving the danger far behind,* he thought.

"Look!" Skyla said.

Up ahead was the shadowy outline of tall trees and an island. As they got closer, Tag saw that the trees had long, twisty black branches. The trees stretched so high that Tag couldn't see their tops.

"We've almost made it!" Tag cried. "Blaze must be somewhere on that island."

"Tag," Skyla whispered, pointing at the water. Small ripples moved across the surface. "There's something down there."

Tag froze. He watched the silvery water as the ripples moved closer and closer. Then—

BANG! Something hard hit the side of the raft.

Tag wobbled, then lost his balance. He fell off the raft and sank into the deep, cold water!

UNDER ATTACK!

Tag struggled to swim up to the surface. His feet squelched in the mud beneath him and his wings caught on twisty tree roots under water. There was darkness everywhere.

Something tugged on his feathers. Tag swam as fast as he could, kicking his feet and flapping his wings. Finally, he saw a circle of light above him: the moon! He flew toward it and burst out of the water.

SWOOSH! Something leaped out of the water behind him. It brushed against his tail feathers.

He flew higher, afraid to look back and see what was in the water. Whatever it was, it felt big!

"Tag!" Skyla cried below him.

Tag swooped over the swamp. He watched the water, looking for whatever had knocked him off the raft.

Skyla was clinging to the top of the raft as it rocked back and forth.

"Tag!" she cried again.

"I'm coming!" Tag said. "Hold on."

Tag tried to fly to her, but the mud and water on his wings were making them heavy. He dropped onto a nearby branch with a **THUD!**

"Over here!" he called to her. "Row over to me."

Skyla spun the raft around with her stick, and pushed toward Tag.

Behind her, the water rippled again. Tag could see a long, dark shape swimming in the swamp. It followed Skyla on the raft, getting closer and closer to her.

Tag pulled out his dagger, but Skyla was too far away, and he still couldn't fly yet.

"Look out behind you!" Tag shouted.

RARGH!

A large head rose from beneath the silver water! It looked like a crocodile, but it was much, much bigger than any Tag had seen before. Its scales were red and purple. Its huge jaws opened wide, ready to bite the raft. Tag gasped at the sight of rows of razor-sharp teeth.

"Tag!" Skyla screamed as she pushed the raft even faster.

Tag reached out and grabbed Skyla's paw.

CHOMP!

The creature's jaws came down on the raft, almost catching Skyla's tail.

Tag pulled Skyla's paw, and they landed in a jumble on a branch.

The creature gave another **CHOMP!** The raft broke into pieces.

Tag threw a nearby stick at the creature's head.

ARGH! The creature howled, then disappeared beneath the silvery water.

THE TALL TREES

"**A**re you okay?" Tag asked.

Skyla nodded. "That was close!" she puffed. "What was that?"

Tag scanned the water. "It looked like some kind of *huge* crocodile," he said. "We need to get out of here in case it comes back."

"Yes," Skyla agreed. "Maybe that creature is what the toads were trying to warn us about?"

"Maybe . . ." Tag said.

They made their way along the branch.

"The water is more shallow down here," Tag told her.

They jumped into the water, and walked toward the island. It rose up out of the water ahead and was covered with tall trees.

"Let's find Blaze and get out of here," Skyla said.

Tag checked his sack to make sure that the map, the Ember Stone, and the feathers were okay after being underwater. The map was a little damp, but he could still see the pictures.

"Come on," he said as they reached the edge of the island. "The tall trees are right ahead!"

Skyla started to run, but then she coughed. "ACK! ACK!"

"Are you okay?" Tag asked.

Skyla waved a paw at him. "I'm fine. Come on, let's go rescue our friend!"

Tag looked up in wonder. The trees towered over them. An enormous nest sat at the end of every branch. But the nests weren't made from twigs and leaves, like Tag's nest. These nests seemed to have grown out of the trees from small twisted branches.

"Wait!" Tag said, holding Skyla's paw.

He pointed up to the nests high above them. Long, brightly colored feathers hung down over the edge, like a long cloak. From far away they almost looked like they could be firehawks. Close-up though, Tag could see that these birds were much, much larger and had curved purple beaks.

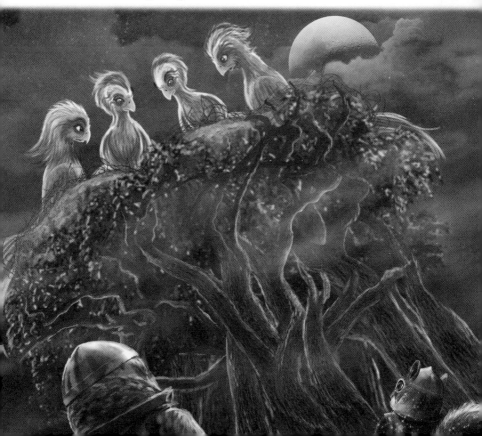

"There's a giant bird inside every nest," Skyla whispered. "How are we going to find Blaze without being seen?"

"The golden feathers showed us that Blaze was in one of these nests," Tag said. "So she must be here somewhere. We are just going to have to wait until the birds leave before we investigate."

Skyla sighed and sat down beneath one of the trees. Tag sat beside her.

"ACK! ACK!" Skyla coughed again.

"Shhh," Tag whispered as he gently covered her mouth with his wing. "We can't let them know we're here."

Skyla nodded.

And they waited.

Suddenly, there was a loud **CAWWWWW!**

Tag and Skyla hid behind a tree trunk.

"Look!" Skyla cried. "The birds are all flying away!"

The giant birds had taken to the air. They followed the largest cawing bird.

"That one looks like their leader," Tag said. "I bet they're going to find food."

Tag and Skyla looked at each other.

"Time to find Blaze!" Skyla said.

THE HIDDEN SURPRISE

As soon as the giant birds were out of sight, Skyla raced up the closest tree to look for Blaze.

Tag took to the sky. He soared over and under the nests, searching everywhere.

Something moved in the nest below him. Tag quickly landed on a branch and hid out of sight. He peeked around some leaves and froze.

Not all the giant birds had left their nests! One of them had stayed behind and was sleeping in the highest nest on the tallest tree.

Tag waved at Skyla and pointed at the nest. Skyla's eyes grew wide. She leaped from branch to branch until she landed beside Tag.

"Do you think that bird stayed behind to guard Blaze?" Skyla whispered.

Tag nodded. "The other nests are empty. Blaze must be in that nest, too."

"Then let's go get her!" Skyla said.

Tag flew to the next branch to get a better look.

ZZZZZZ!

The giant bird was snoring. Tag could not see any sign of Blaze.

I need to get closer, he thought.

Tag shuffled slowly along the branch. He moved closer, closer, closer to the nest. The giant bird was even bigger than Tag had thought. Its beak was as big as he was!

Tag gulped as he took a step closer to peek inside the nest.

Suddenly, the giant bird ruffled its big feathers. Tag jumped! He almost slipped off the branch, but held tight with his talons.

"Blaze!" he whispered toward the nest. "Are you in there?"

There was no reply. The giant bird snored softly.

"Blaze?" Tag called again, a little louder. "It's me, Tag."

"Mmmmfffff!" a voice replied.

The giant bird ruffled its feathers again.

But Tag had recognized that voice! Hope rose in his chest. Then he spotted a smaller bunch of feathers beneath the giant bird!

It was Blaze!

THE RESCUE

"**M**mmmffff!" Blaze called from deep within the nest.

"Stay calm and quiet," Tag told her. "We're going to save you."

He flew to Skyla on the branch above.

"Blaze is trapped in that nest beneath the sleeping bird!" he told her.

Skyla and Tag peered down at the nest below. The giant bird's long feathers covered Blaze.

"How are we going to get Blaze out of there?" Skyla asked.

"I don't know," Tag replied. "But that bird is not going anywhere, at least not until the others come back. And then there will be too many of them for us to rescue Blaze."

"We have to get her out of there now," Skyla said.

"I have an idea! Follow me," Tag said.

He flew to the nest, and Skyla followed. Tag hopped to where Blaze's wing was peeking out beneath one of the giant bird's heavy wings.

ZZZZZZ! The giant bird continued to snore.

"I'll gently lift the giant bird's wing," Tag whispered to Skyla. "You try and pull Blaze free."

Carefully, Tag lifted up the giant bird's wing and crept beneath its huge feathers. He held the wing up above his head with his own shaky wings.

"Peep!" Blaze called.

"Shh!" Tag whispered. "Can you get out?"

Blaze nodded.

Tag's feathers trembled as Skyla climbed into the nest. She helped Tag hold up the giant bird's heavy wing. Slowly, Blaze wriggled her body to try to get out from under the giant bird. Then she stopped.

"Keep going! You're almost out," Tag said.

Blaze shook her head. "My tail feathers are stuck."

"I'll help," Skyla whispered. She squeezed her way farther into the nest, getting closer to the giant bird.

Tag held his breath. Then, with a soft *peep*, Blaze wriggled free!

Skyla hurried out of the nest and gave Blaze a hug. Tag carefully lowered the giant bird's wing and joined Skyla and Blaze in a big hug.

"Thank you!" Blaze cried. "I knew you'd find me!"

"We have to go before this bird wakes up," Tag said. "Blaze, can you fly?"

Blaze grinned. "Get on my back, Skyla," she said.

Together again, the three friends soared away from the tall trees.

They landed at the edge of the island.

"I think we're safe here," Tag said. He gave Blaze some water and berries—and another hug. "We've missed you!"

"Why did the giant birds take you?" Skyla asked.

"I think they thought I was their baby," Blaze said.

SNARL!

Just then, a huge creature roared out of the water! It crawled toward them, through the mud.

"This is the same creature that attacked us earlier!" Tag cried.

They could see the creature clearly now. It had small wings on its back, like a dragon. And the end of its tail was as sharp and pointed as a sword.

"That's no ordinary crocodile," Blaze said. "It's some sort of croco-dragon!"

Tag and Skyla pulled out their weapons as Blaze's feathers lit up one by one.

"Get ready to fight!" Tag said.

THE CROCO-
DRAGON

Tthe enormous croco-dragon's bright eyes
glared at the friends as it crept closer to them.
It snapped its sharp teeth at the friends.

Skyla leaped through the air, shooting acorns at the croco-dragon's head.

Tag followed, flying at the creature with his dagger held high.

The croco-dragon roared and opened its huge jaws. A blast of green fire shot out of its mouth.

Tag was knocked to the ground.

Skyla shot more acorns at the creature, but it sent out another blast of green fire and burned the nuts to ash.

"My tail!" Skyla cried as burning green fire caught the tip of her tail.

Tag quickly scooped up some mud and covered his friend's tail. The fire went out.

Blaze's feathers glowed brighter. She shot a huge fireball at the croco-dragon, but the flames bounced off its tough skin.

"The creature is too strong!" Skyla cried.

"Fly away!" Tag shouted.

Blaze's feathers returned to normal and Skyla jumped on her back. They followed Tag into the sky, but—

The croco-dragon followed! It chased after them, flapping its small wings. Whichever way they turned, the creature followed, blasting green fire.

"My wings are so tired!" Tag called to his friends. "I need to land!"

He landed in a muddy puddle. Blaze and Skyla landed beside him.

They watched as the croco-dragon landed a little way ahead. It roared, then crept toward them, preparing to attack.

"We have to do something!" Skyla said. "Try your firehawk cry, Blaze!"

Blaze opened her beak. But before she could make a sound, a dark shadow fell over them. The croco-dragon's eyes went wide. It walked backward, looking frightened.

Before Tag knew what had happened, the creature dived into the Silver Swamp and disappeared beneath the water.

The friends froze. Something new crept up behind them, blocking the moon's light. Darkness surrounded them. Tag slowly turned to see what was making the dark shadow.

Standing tall in front of them was something even more terrifying than the croco-dragon: it was Thorn!

AN OLD ENEMY

Tag's wings shook as he stared up at Thorn. He held out his dagger.

Tag, Blaze, and Skyla had helped stop the evil vulture's plan to destroy the enchanted land of Perodia. Now, it seemed, he had come after them for revenge!

"I knew someone was following us!" Tag cried. "I should have known it was *you*, Thorn!"

Tag thought of all the times he had seen the dark smudge on the map and the dark figure in the trees. He gripped his sack tighter, knowing the Ember Stone was still safely inside.

He must have followed us into the Cloud Kingdom, Tag thought. *I'm not letting him get his claws on the stone!*

Blaze stepped forward, her wings glowing. She looked angry.

"Wait!" the vulture said, holding out his wings. "It's not what you think."

"So you *haven't* been following us?" asked Tag.

The vulture looked at the ground. "Well, I have been following you. But not to hurt you. And I am not Thorn. I'm his twin brother, Claw."

"Ha!" Tag laughed. "How can we believe you?"

The vulture limped over to stand right before the friends.

Blaze frowned as she eyed Claw. "Thorn didn't have a bad leg," she said slowly.

Claw smiled at Blaze. "When Thorn attacked the firehawks on Fire Island, I tried to help them. I am not like my brother," he explained. "I have no powers. Thorn wanted me to become one of his spies. But I did not want to see Perodia destroyed. When firehawks opened the portal to the Cloud Kingdom, I followed them. But when we arrived, the firehawks disappeared. I was trapped here! There is no way out of the Cloud Kingdom without magic! When I saw Blaze—a firehawk—I thought you might be

able to go home."

Blaze nodded. "I know how it feels to be trapped," she said.

Tag looked at Skyla and Blaze. Claw didn't know that they had their own magic to get back to Perodia—the Ember Stone and the golden feathers.

"Can I travel with you?" Claw asked. "If I stay with you, we might find a portal together. Please, I just want to find a way back home."

Tag remembered what Claw had said about following the firehawks into the Cloud Kingdom. *Maybe Claw could lead us to the firehawks*, he thought. A plan began to form in his head.

But can we trust Claw? he wondered, looking into the vulture's eyes.

CHAPTER 12

POISONED!

"We have to talk," Tag told Skyla and Blaze. He pulled them away from Claw.

"Claw doesn't know about the golden feathers or the Ember Stone," Tag said. He watched the vulture out of the corner of his eye. "But he *does* know where the firehawks were in the Cloud Kingdom."

Blaze grinned. "And if he takes us there, maybe we will find another portal that will lead us to them!" she said excitedly.

"Exactly!" Tag said. "What do you think, Skyla?"

Skyla tried to answer, but she could only cough. "ACK! ACK!"

"Are you okay?" Tag asked.

Skyla nodded. "We should get out of here," she said quietly. "Before the giant birds notice that Blaze is gone."

"Don't tell Claw about the golden feathers," Blaze whispered to her friends. "Or the Ember Stone."

They all nodded in agreement.

"ACK ACK!" Skyla coughed again.

Blaze looked worried. "Are you sick?" she asked.

"No, don't worry about me," Skyla replied. "It's just a small cough. Maybe I'm allergic to something in the Cloud Kingdom."

The friends walked back toward Claw.

"Claw," Tag said. "We don't trust you. But you can come with us."

Claw gave Tag a small smile. "Thank you," he said.

Then the four of them took to the sky and soared over the Silver Swamp. The swamp's silvery water sparkled in the moonlight.

This time it didn't take them long to reach land on the other side.

As they landed, it was like a light had been switched on.

"It's so bright!" Blaze said.

Tag looked up. In a flash, the dark sky had gone. Now there was only bright sunshine. Tag was glad to leave the dark swamp far behind.

"We should check the map," Tag said. "It might show us which way to go next."

Claw gave Tag a strange look. "You have a magic map?" he asked.

Tag shook his head quickly. "Just an ordinary map," he lied.

But when he peered at the map, it was blank!

That's strange, Tag thought. He put the map away quickly so that Claw couldn't see what was . . . *or wasn't* . . . on it.

"What do you know about the portals?" Blaze asked Claw.

"They are created from magical objects, like the golden tail feathers that all firehawks have," Claw told Blaze.

Blaze frowned. "I don't have them," she said.

"Not yet. But you are still a young firehawk. Your tail feathers will grow," Claw said. "Maybe we could find another magical object. Like a *stone* perhaps?"

"ACK!"

Skyla coughed again. Her face looked grayer than usual.

"Skyla?" Tag asked.

Suddenly, Skyla swayed from side to side. Then she fell to the ground!

Blaze lifted Skyla up and hugged her close. "What's wrong with her?" she asked.

Claw brushed the tip of his wing over Skyla's face. His feathers came away covered in purple glitter.

"Did she touch a tall, bell-shaped flower?" Claw asked.

"Yes," Tag said. "It shot out glitter at her."

"That glitter is poisonous!" Claw cried, quickly brushing it off of his wing.

Tag gasped. "*That's* what the toads saw! They saw the glitter! They were trying to tell us Skyla was in danger!"

"If you want to save your friend's life, we will have to move quickly," Claw said. "And you will *have* to trust me."

THE HEALING POOL

Tag didn't trust Claw, but Skyla was getting sicker and sicker by the minute. He didn't have a choice. "Okay, let's go," Tag said.

Skyla opened her eyes and groaned.

Blaze held her paw. "Try to rest," she told her. "We're going to make you better."

Tag helped Skyla onto Blaze's back.

"Hold on," Tag told her.

They took off, following Claw over the forest. The trees below shimmered, reminding Tag of the nixies' sparkly magic.

"Down there!" Claw called.

Tag soared to the ground. Blaze landed next to him, carefully holding Skyla. They were in another small clearing surrounded by tall, shiny grass.

"This grass isn't poisonous, is it?" Tag asked, being careful not to touch it.

"No," Claw said. "Hurry! Bring Skyla this way."

Claw moved the tall grass aside to reveal a hidden pool. It was surrounded by rocks that sparkled like diamonds.

"What is that?" Blaze asked, staring at the pool.

Tag put the tip of his wing into the pool. His wing glowed with a bright light. The water in the pool didn't feel like water. It felt like soft, warm feathers. It felt like home.

"Put Skyla into the pool," Claw ordered.

"Are you sure this will help her?" Tag asked.

The pool didn't seem dangerous, but every time he looked at Claw he saw Thorn's evil eyes looking back at him.

Skyla groaned.

"We have to try," Blaze said.

Together, Tag and Blaze gently put Skyla into the pool.

"She's not going to like this," said Blaze. "Skyla hates water."

"I don't think this pool is filled with water," Tag said.

"You're right," Claw said. "This is a magic pool, full of healing magic."

The three of them watched Skyla float in the pool. Skyla lay very still. They waited. Then suddenly—

Her fur rippled. Slowly, Skyla's soft gray fur turned red, then green, then orange, then purple. She looked like a giant blueberry!

Clouds of glitter shot out of Skyla's mouth as she coughed.

"She's getting worse, not better!" Tag shouted at Claw. "You tricked us!"

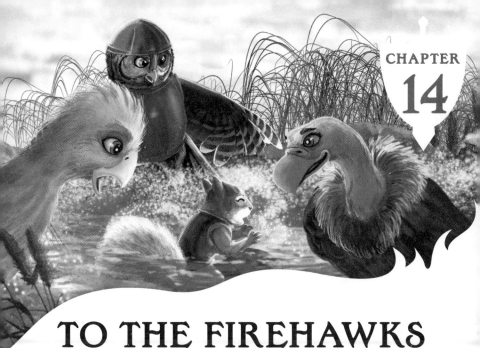

TO THE FIREHAWKS

"**D**o something!" Blaze shouted at Claw.

"There's nothing I can do," Claw replied.

Blaze gave Tag a worried look. "What now?" she asked.

"You'll have to trust me," Claw said. "Just wait . . ."

Tag watched. His heart thumped in his chest as he waited for the magic to work.

Suddenly, Skyla twitched and then slowly opened her eyes.

"Tag?" Skyla whispered.

"Skyla!" Blaze cried, hugging her friend tight.

Tag helped her out of the pool. The tips of her tail and her ears were still a little purple, but she had stopped coughing. Skyla looked like herself again.

"Are you okay?" Tag asked.

Skyla frowned at her purple tail, then nodded. "I think so. Will my tail stay this color? It looks good!"

Tag looked at the pool. It was now filled with swirling purple glitter.

"Your tail will return to its normal color in time," Claw replied.

"Thank you, Claw," Skyla said. "You saved me."

Claw smiled at Skyla.

Tag turned to his friends. "What do we do now?" he asked.

We can't use the golden feathers or the map, he thought to himself. *We have to keep them a secret.*

"Blaze still needs to find her family," Skyla said.

"Claw," Tag said. "Do you know where the firehawks went to?"

"No," Claw said. "But I think I might know how to find them."

Blaze narrowed her eyes. "I thought you were trapped here," she said. "If you know where they are, why haven't you found them already?"

"The firehawks have left the Cloud Kingdom. And without a magic object, I am trapped here," Claw replied. "But you are not. Blaze is a firehawk. Maybe she can find a way to open another portal. Then we can leave here and find the firehawks, and they can help us get back to Perodia."

"The Cloud Kingdom is so big," Blaze said. "The portal could be anywhere."

"Not anywhere," Claw said. "I can take you to the last place I saw the firehawks."

Tag looked at Skyla, and she nodded. Blaze nodded too.

"Okay," Tag said. "But we will be watching you closely. No evil tricks."

"No tricks," Claw agreed.

"We should rest before we go," Tag said. "Even though the sun is up."

He handed out water, nuts, and berries to Claw and his friends.

Can we really trust Claw? Tag wondered as they built their nests.

He laid down to rest. "Where will we go next?" Tag asked.

"West," Claw replied. "To the Golden Temple."

Tag looked to his friends. Skyla and Blaze were curled up in a nest, their eyes wide open.

"Let's get some sleep," Tag told them. "Tomorrow we're going to find Blaze's family."

ABOUT THE AUTHOR

KATRINA CHARMAN has wanted to be a children's book writer ever since she was eleven, when her teacher asked her class to write an epilogue to Roald Dahl's *Matilda*. Katrina's teacher thought her writing was good enough to send to Roald Dahl himself! Sadly, she never got a reply, but this experience ignited her love of reading and writing. Katrina lives in England with her husband and three daughters. The Last Firehawk is her first early chapter book series in the U.S.

ABOUT THE ILLUSTRATOR

JUDIT TONDORA was born in Hungary and now works from her countryside studio. Her illustrations are rooted in the traditional European style but also contain elements of American mainstream style. Her characters have a vivacious retro vibe placed right into the present day: she says "I put the good old retro together with modern style to give charisma to my illustrations."

Questions and Activities

1. What happens to the sky when Tag and Skyla enter the Silver Swamp? How does this connect to Tag's magical map?

2. How do the toads react when they see Skyla? Why do they react this way?

3. Reread page 70. What are three things we learn about Claw?

4. The friends don't know if they can trust Claw. How does Claw try to show that he can be trusted?

5. Tag and Skyla meet a croco-dragon: It is half crocodile, half dragon. Combine two creatures to create your own Cloud Kingdom creature! Draw and name it.